Mr Biff
the
Boxer

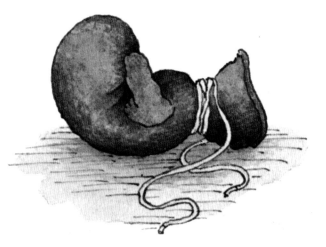

Janet & Allan Ahlberg

PUFFIN BOOKS
Published by the Penguin Group: London, New York, Australia,
Canada, India, Ireland, New Zealand and South Africa
Penguin Books Ltd, Registered Offices:
80 Strand, London WC2R 0RL, England

puffinbooks.com

First published by Viking 1980
Published in Puffin Books 1980
Published in this edition 2013
002
Copyright © Janet and Allan Ahlberg, 1980
All rights reserved
Educational Advisory Editor: Brian Thompson
The moral right of the author and illustrator has been asserted
Printed and bound in China
ISBN: 978-0-723-27558-9

There was once a man named Mr Bop.

Mr Bop was a boxer.

He was as fit as a fiddle.

He was the toughest man in the town.

He was the champion.

There was another boxer in the town.

His name was Mr Biff.

Mr Biff was not as fit as a fiddle.
He ate too many cream cakes.
He drank too many bottles of beer.
Mr Biff was not tough.
He liked to sit in an easy chair
by a cosy fire.
He liked to put his slippers on
and read the paper.
He slept in a feather bed.

One day posters appeared in
the town. They said:

BIG CHARITY FIGHT
MR BIFF AGAINST MR BOP

Bonzo Biff shared a bone with
the Bop dog.
And a happy time was had by all.

The End